SMOKEY THE BEAR

BY JANE WERNER

PICTURES BY
RICHARD SCARRY

GOLDEN PLEASURE BOOKS

LONDON

GOLDEN PLEASURE BOOKS LTD

WESTBOOK HOUSE · FULHAM BROADWAY · LONDON

© Copyright Golden Pleasure Books Ltd. 1955 and 1960
Printed in Czechoslovakia

IT WAS a bright May morning in the mountain forest
of New Mexico. Bear Cub followed his mother out into
the sunshine. He sniffed the hot, dry, pine-smelling air.

This was Bear Cub's first spring. He was still young, and he had a lot to learn. Mother Bear was busy teaching him how to choose the tastiest berries, where to find clear drinking water, how to turn over a log to uncover a nice meal of bugs.

Most important, his mother taught him: "When danger threatens, climb a tree!"

One day Bear Cub and his mother were out hunting tasty berries. Suddenly Bear Cub's mother stopped and sniffed. Bear Cub sniffed, too. There was something strange in the air. His eyes smarted.

And off in the distance he heard a great roaring
sound, like all the winds blowing together through the
tops of the tall pines.

Bear Cub rubbed his eyes with his paws, but they still smarted. And now a thick blackness was creeping toward them through the branches of the trees.

All the creatures of the woods were fleeing from the
roaring darkness—the deer and the squirrels, the
rabbits and the birds.

"Hurry, hurry!" the birds were screaming as they flew. Mother Bear pushed Bear Cub along ahead of her as fast as his feet could go. But it was not fast enough. The thick smoke caught up with them.

Bear Cub could not hear his mother's voice behind him. When he turned he could not see her.

Bear Cub was frightened. What should he do? Then he remembered. "When danger threatens," his mother had taught him, "climb a tree."

So up a pine tree Bear Cub went. Around him the forest fire roared and crackled. Flames licked at Bear Cub's shaggy fur and singed his tender paws. But he closed his eyes and just hung on.

When he opened his eyes again after a while, he could scarcely believe what he saw. Instead of the cool, green, shady woods, all around him stood hundreds of ugly blackened sticks with trails of smoke still curling from them. Suddenly he heard a friendly voice.

It was a fire-fighting forest ranger. The ranger reached up and took Bear Cub into his arms. "What's your name, fellow—Smokey?" From then on it was.

Though Smokey could not understand the words, he knew the voice was kind. He knew the water from the ranger's canteen felt wet and cool in his dry throat.

He knew the food from the ranger's pack tasted fine, and felt just fine in his hollow insides. He knew the salve and bandages made his burned paws feel good again.

Then the ranger took Smokey to the game warden's home. He liked to sit with the family and play with their little girl.

"I wish every boy and girl could meet Smokey," said the State Game Warden. "He'd teach them how extra important it is to be careful of fires in the woods."

"Good idea!" said another. "The best place for him to meet boys and girls is in a zoo."

So into a plane went Smokey the Bear, and away he flew to Washington, D.C., where he lives in the wonderful National Zoo. Every day there he meets boys and girls from all over the country.

He likes them to join his Junior Forest Rangers, to help him prevent terrible forest fires, like the one that destroyed his home.

These are their easy rules:

Remind your parents and friends to . . .
Break matches in two. When they can hold the
burned end between their fingers, no fire is left.

Crush out cigaretes,
then use the ash tray.

Drown campfires; then stir the ashes to make sure they are out.

Never burn grass, brush, or rubbish on windy days.
When they do burn it, they should have plenty of
help.

Smokey

and His Animal Friends

BY CHARLES SPAIN VERRAL
PICTURES BY MEL CRAWFORD

Smokey the Bear was worried. It was his job to guard the forest against fire. And it was also his job to look after all the animals and birds of the forest.

And now one of the animals had disappeared.

The rabbits were the first to tell him about it. Then
the birds. Then the squirrels and the chipmunks and
all the small creatures of the woods told him.

A terrible thing had happened.

That morning a little fawn, named Fern, had been out for a walk with her mother. Suddenly a dog had come barking after them, and the mother deer had hidden Fern behind a log. Then she had let the dog chase her to the far side of the woods. She had done this on purpose to keep her fawn safe from harm.

But by the time she got back to the log, Fern had disappeared.

The mother deer showed Smokey where she had hidden Fern.

Smokey examined the ground. He saw a few tiny hoof marks. But they stopped suddenly.

Smokey was worried. The forest was full of dangers for a baby fawn. There were big, hungry animals like the mountain lion.

And even worse, there might be a forest fire, from which all the animals would have to flee.

He'd have to find Fern somehow—before it was too late.

Smokey called the birds together.

"Search the forest from the sky," he told them.

"Then report to me."

The birds flew away.

Smokey gathered around him the rabbits and the squirrels and the chipmunks and all the small creatures of the woods.

"Look under every bush and in every hollow in the forest," he told them. "Then report to me."

The rabbits and the squirrels and the chipmunks, the fox and the porcupines and the raccoons—all the small creatures of the woods scampered away.

After a while the birds came back.
They had seen no sign of the fawn.

The rabbits and the squirrels and all the small
creatures of the woods returned.
They had found no trace of Fern.

Then Willy, the porcupine, came waddling up.
He hadn't seen Fern but he'd seen something else.
He'd seen Snarler, the mountain lion, in the hills back
of the woods.

Smokey was very worried when he heard this.
Snarler was always hungry.

"I'm going to talk to Snarler," Smokey said.

The animals and the birds told Smokey not to go.
But Smokey went anyway. He climbed right up to
the mountain lion's den.

"Tell me, Snarler, have you seen Fern the fawn?"
Smokey asked.

Snarler didn't answer. He only gave a bad-tempered
growl and told Smokey to go away.

"I don't think Snarler harmed Fern," Smokey said to the animals and the birds when he got back. "He's much too thin and cross to have eaten for some time. But where could that fawn have gone?"

Just then, from away off, Smokey heard a dog barking.

"That sounds like Spot, the farm dog," said Smokey.

Smokey jumped up from the stump where he had been sitting. It must have been Spot who had chased the mother deer.

"Why didn't I think of that before?" Smokey said. "I'll go to the farm and question Spot. Perhaps he might know why the fawn has disappeared."

Smokey set off through the woods.

When he reached the farm, Smokey saw Spot bounding across the barnyard. He was following the farmer's children, Roy and Sue, into the barn.

Smokey walked over to the barn.

Inside he heard Sue's voice. "Here's your bottle, baby. Now drink all of it."

Smokey peeked through the doorway and was he surprised! For Sue was feeding the bottle—not to a baby—but to a fawn. It was Fern!

Smokey stepped into the barn.

"Don't be afraid," he said. "I think you know me."

"Why, you're Smokey the Bear!" Roy said. "I've seen your picture on posters."

"What are you doing here, Smokey?" Sue asked. "We're always careful with our camp fires, and Daddy is careful, too, when he's burning things around the farm."

"I know, Sue," said Smokey. "I was looking for that fawn."

"We found her in the woods. Her mother must have left her to die. So we brought her home," Roy said.

"The doe didn't leave her fawn to die," Smokey said. "It was her way of keeping the young one safe from your dog. Now I must take Fern back to her mother and her home in the woods."

"But the fawn's our pet," Sue said. "We'll feed her and look after her. She'll be happy here."

Smokey shook his head.

"That's a mistake many people make," he said. "Wild animals aren't happy with humans. They belong in the woods. That's their home. Ask any forest ranger or game warden. They'll tell you the same thing....Now come along. We'll all take Fern back."

Roy and Sue didn't want to give up their pet. But they went with Smokey and Fern into the cool green woods.

And when the twins saw the fawn run to her mother, and when they heard the big welcome the animals and the birds gave Fern, Roy and Sue knew that Smokey had been right.

The forest is a fawn's real home. And for an animal or a bird or a boy or a girl, home is the best place in the world to be.